THE ELEPHANT WHO LIKED TO SMASH SMALL CARS

BY JEAN MERRILL AND RONNI SOLBERT

The New York Review Children's Collection

THIS IS A NEW YORK REVIEW BOOK
PUBLISHED BY THE NEW YORK REVIEW OF BOOKS
435 Hudson Street, New York, NY 10014
www.nyrb.com

Library of Congress Cataloging-in-Publication Data
Merrill, Jean, author.
The elephant who liked to smash small cars / by Jean Merrill and Ronni Solbert.
pages cm. — (New York Review Books Children's Collection)
Originally published: New York : Pantheon Books, © 1967.
Summary: An elephant who likes to smash small cars is taught a lesson by a car salesman.
ISBN 978-1-59017-872-0 (alk. paper)
1. Elephants—Juvenile fiction. 2. Sales personnel—Juvenile fiction. 3. Conduct of life—Juvenile fiction.
[1. Elephants—Fiction. 2. Automobiles—Fiction. 3. Conduct of life—Fiction.] I. Solbert, Ronni, illustrator. II. Title.
III. Series: New York Review children's collection.
PZ7.M54535El 2015
[E]—dc23
                                                2014036294

ISBN 978-1-59017-872-0

Cover design by Louise Fili Ltd.

Printed in the United States on acid-free paper.
2 4 6 8 10 9 7 5 3 1

for Tony Scott

There was an elephant who liked to smash small cars.

Every time a small car came along
the road where the elephant lived,
the elephant would jump on the car.

He would jump up and down on it
until he smashed it.

He smashed a small red car.

He smashed a small blue car.

He smashed a small yellow car.
All the time he was smashing cars,
the elephant sang a little song:

Smashing cars! Smashing cars!
How I love to smash small cars!

The Smashing Song

Sma-shing cars! Sma-shing cars!

How I love to smash small cars!

One day, a car salesman opened a car store
on the road where the elephant lived.

The man had a lot of small cars to sell.

The elephant came along and said,
"I wouldn't open a car store here,
if I were you."
"Why not?" said the salesman.
"I like to smash small cars," said
the elephant. "That's why."

The elephant sang the car salesman
his little song:

Smashing cars! Smashing cars!
How I love to smash small cars!

And then he began jumping up and
down on all the man's small cars.

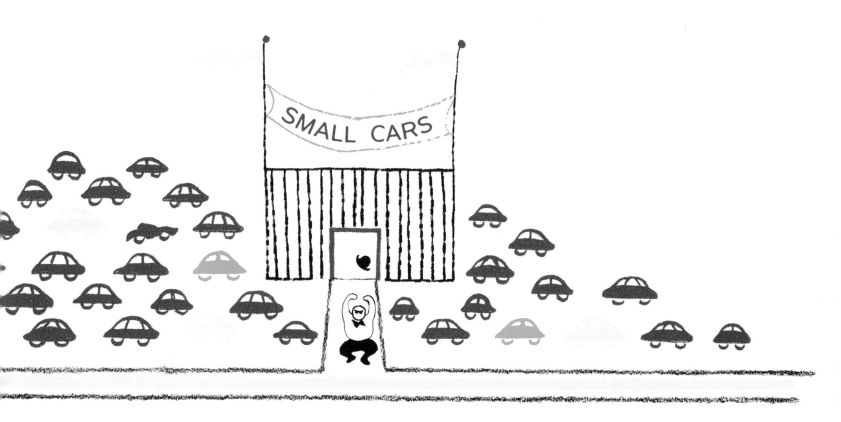

He smashed one.
He smashed two.
He smashed three.

He smashed them ALL.

So the salesman said, "I guess I won't
sell small cars. I have a better idea."

The next day, the elephant came down
the road, and what did he see?
Big cars!

The man had a lot of big cars to sell.
There were big red cars, big blue cars,
big yellow cars, and big black cars.

"Hey," said the elephant.
"What's the big idea?"

"I'm going to sell big cars," said the car salesman. "They are very good for smashing elephants."

The man jumped into a big red car
and smashed the elephant right into
a tree.

"Stop!" cried the elephant, before he
was smashed absolutely flat.
The man stopped before the elephant
was smashed absolutely flat.

Then the man jumped into a big blue
car and smashed the elephant right into
a house.

"Stop!" cried the elephant, before he
was smashed absolutely flat.

The man stopped to sing a little song.
He sang:

Smashing's fun! Smashing's fun!
Smashing elephants is fun!

And then the man jumped into a very
big black car and smashed the elephant
so hard that he flew high into the sky.

The elephant fell down into a lake.

"I don't think big cars are a good idea,"
the elephant said to the salesman.
"Why don't you sell small cars?"
"I would," said the salesman,
"if you wouldn't smash them all."
So the elephant said he wouldn't.

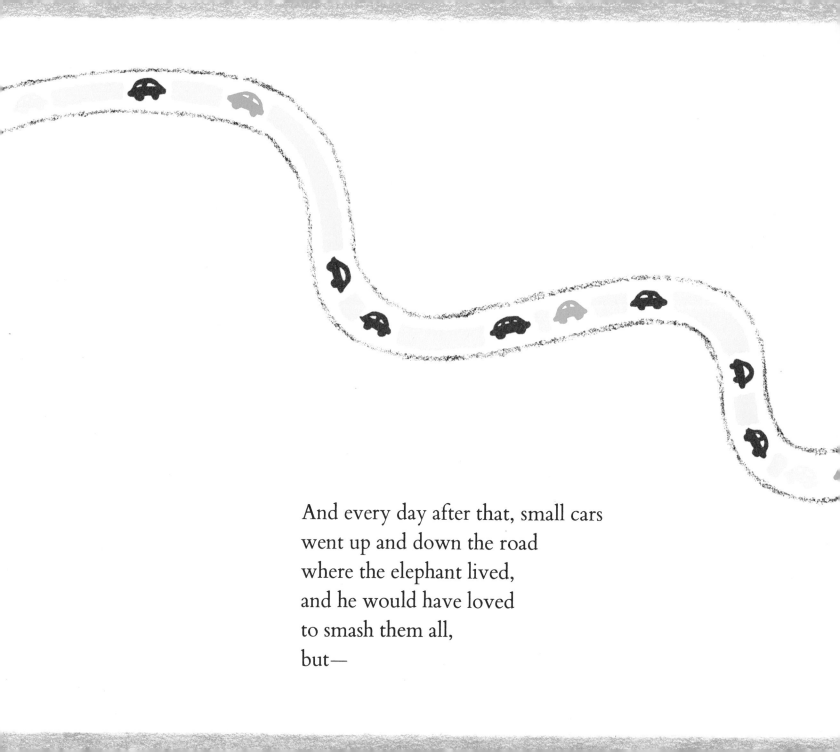

And every day after that, small cars
went up and down the road
where the elephant lived,
and he would have loved
to smash them all,
but—

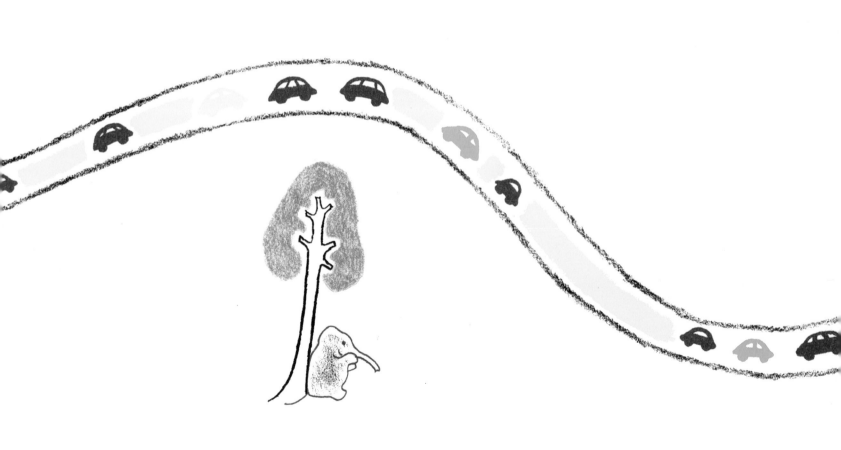

HE DIDN'T.

JEAN MERRILL (1923–2012) was born in Rochester, New York, and grew up on a dairy and apple farm near Lake Ontario. She received a master's degree in English literature from Wellesley in 1945 and later studied folklore in India on a Fulbright fellowship. She worked for many years as an editor at *Scholastic Magazine*, *Literary Cavalcade*, and the publications department of Bank Street College before turning to writing full time. Her first book, *Henry, the Hand-Painted Mouse*, was published in 1951 and her last, *The Girl Who Loved Caterpillars: A Twelfth-Century Tale from Japan*, in 1992. In between she wrote some thirty books for young readers, including *The Pushcart War* (1964; available from The New York Review Children's Collection), *The Elephant Who Liked to Smash Small Cars* (1967), and *The Toothpaste Millionaire* (1977).

RONNI SOLBERT (b. 1925) was born in Washington, D.C., and graduated from Vassar and the Cranbrook Academy of Art. As a Fulbright recipient she studied folk and tribal art in India. She has illustrated more than forty children's books and written and illustrated three of her own. As a painter, sculptor, and photographer she has exhibited widely in the United States and abroad.

TITLES IN THE NEW YORK REVIEW CHILDREN'S COLLECTION

ESTHER AVERILL
Captains of the City Streets
The Hotel Cat
Jenny and the Cat Club
Jenny Goes to Sea
Jenny's Birthday Book
Jenny's Moonlight Adventure
The School for Cats

JAMES CLOYD BOWMAN
Pecos Bill: The Greatest Cowboy of All Time

PALMER BROWN
Beyond the Pawpaw Trees
Cheerful
Hickory
The Silver Nutmeg
Something for Christmas

SHEILA BURNFORD
Bel Ria: Dog of War

DINO BUZZATI
The Bears' Famous Invasion of Sicily

MARY CHASE
Loretta Mason Potts

CARLO COLLODI and FULVIO TESTA
Pinocchio

INGRI and EDGAR PARIN D'AULAIRE
D'Aulaires' Book of Animals
D'Aulaires' Book of Norse Myths
D'Aulaires' Book of Trolls
Foxie: The Singing Dog
The Terrible Troll-Bird
Too Big
The Two Cars

EILÍS DILLON
The Island of Horses
The Lost Island

ELEANOR FARJEON
The Little Bookroom

PENELOPE FARMER
Charlotte Sometimes

PAUL GALLICO
The Abandoned

LEON GARFIELD
The Complete Bostock and Harris
Smith: The Story of a Pickpocket

RUMER GODDEN
An Episode of Sparrows
The Mousewife

MARIA GRIPE and HARALD GRIPE
The Glassblower's Children

LUCRETIA P. HALE
The Peterkin Papers

RUSSELL and LILLIAN HOBAN
The Sorely Trying Day

RUTH KRAUSS and MARC SIMONT
The Backward Day

DOROTHY KUNHARDT
Junket Is Nice
Now Open the Box

MUNRO LEAF and ROBERT LAWSON
Wee Gillis

RHODA LEVINE and EDWARD GOREY
He Was There from the Day We Moved In
Three Ladies Beside the Sea

BETTY JEAN LIFTON and EIKOH HOSOE
Taka-chan and I

NORMAN LINDSAY
The Magic Pudding

ERIC LINKLATER
The Wind on the Moon

J. P. MARTIN
Uncle
Uncle Cleans Up

JOHN MASEFIELD
The Box of Delights
The Midnight Folk

WILLIAM McCLEERY and WARREN CHAPPELL
Wolf Story

JEAN MERRILL and RONNI SOLBERT
The Elephant Who Liked to Smash Small Cars
The Pushcart War

E. NESBIT
The House of Arden

ALFRED OLLIVANT'S
Bob, Son of Battle: The Last Gray Dog of Kenmuir
A New Version by LYDIA DAVIS

DANIEL PINKWATER
Lizard Music

OTFRIED PREUSSLER
Krabat & the Sorcerer's Mill

VLADIMIR RADUNSKY and CHRIS RASCHKA
Alphabetabum

ALASTAIR REID and BOB GILL
Supposing…

ALASTAIR REID and BEN SHAHN
Ounce Dice Trice

BARBARA SLEIGH
Carbonel and Calidor
Carbonel: The King of the Cats
The Kingdom of Carbonel

E. C. SPYKMAN
Terrible, Horrible Edie

FRANK TASHLIN
The Bear That Wasn't

VAL TEAL and ROBERT LAWSON
The Little Woman Wanted Noise

JAMES THURBER
The 13 Clocks
The Wonderful O

ALISON UTTLEY
A Traveller in Time

T. H. WHITE
Mistress Masham's Repose

MARJORIE WINSLOW and ERIK BLEGVAD
Mud Pies and Other Recipes

REINER ZIMNIK
The Bear and the People